To Helen, Charlotte, Sharon,
Vincent, Laura, Eilidh
and Mhairi. Your
friendship really is the
best of presents!
Neil x

Red Robin Books is an imprint of Corner To Learn Limited

Published by
Corner To Learn Limited
Willow Cottage • 26 Purton Stoke
Swindon • Wiltshire SN5 4JF • UK

ISBN: 978-1-908702-06-7

First published in the UK 2012
Text © Neil Griffiths 2012
Illustrations © Melanie Siegel 2012

Design by David Rose

Printed in China

The Best Present Ever!

Neil Griffiths

Illustrated by **Melanie Siegel**

Once upon a time, long, long ago, in a land far, far away lived a kind and generous King and Queen.

The King and Queen loved each other very much as they did each and every person in their kingdom.

Such was their kindness, that each and every day they would be found somewhere in the kingdom giving out presents.

No one was ever forgotten (as the present list officer kept a list!).

They knew everyone's birthday and anniversaries and, of course, Christmas was simply presents, presents, presents! In fact, they loved to give presents more than anything else.

Each present was always beautifully wrapped (with the help of the royal wrappers!) and a neat name label placed on it (thanks to the royal neat name writers!). What a happy land it was!

But one morning, the Queen was to bring news that made everyone even happier! She announced to the King that she had a present for him and it was to be the best present he had ever had!

But what could it be? The King tried to guess.
"Was it a new crown?" he asked.
"No," said the Queen,
"you already have lots in
the Royal Jewels Room."

"Was it new shoes?"
he tried to guess.
"No!" sighed the Queen.
"When you already
have 412 pairs!"
"Really!" he gasped.

"A new throne!" he exclaimed.
"No!" she sighed again. "You
already have the finest
throne ever made!"
"Then tell me, tell me!"
whined the King.

"We are going to have a baby!" she beamed.
"A b-b-b-b-baby!" stuttered the King in amazement.
"Yes," said the Queen proudly.

"A baby, a baby! We are to have a baby! I'm to be a father!" shouted the King at the top of his voice as he danced with happiness around the palace.

News quickly spread throughout the kingdom
and cheering could be heard all day and night.
In fact, everyone gave each other
presents to celebrate
the wonderful news.

But what present could the King give the Queen? They had longed for a baby and the King wanted to give his wife a present to show how happy he was. But this had to be the best present he had ever given her. Messengers were sent out in search of the finest gift fit for the Queen.

After several days, merchants arrived at the
royal palace in hope that the King would
choose their riches as a gift for the Queen.
From Africa came dazzling diamonds that
caught the sunlight.
Everyone went "Oooh!"

From China came sumptuous silks that slid smoothly across the skin. Everyone went "Aah!"

From Russia came gleaming gold that glowed like fire. Everyone went "Uuh!" Which would the King choose?

He was just about to make his mind up when a young
fisherman came rushing in dragging an old sack.
The palace courtiers stuck their noses in the air with disgust.
Fancy bringing a grubby old sack into the palace.
"Outrageous!" they all muttered.
"Your Majesty. Please wait," he pleaded.
"I have a gift for the Queen."

With that, he untied the sack and out poured dozens of dirty shells! Everyone gasped and then burst into uncontrollable laughter. "How could he offer such a ghastly gift?" they all thought.

But the King was both kind and wise and he silenced the palace and asked the fisherman to explain himself. "Your Majesty, they may seem on the outside an ugly gift unworthy of a Queen so beautiful. But hidden inside is a secret surprise that is smoother than silk, glows brighter than gold, holds the colours of the rainbow and will dazzle you more than any diamond," he announced.

Tittering could be heard from the gathering
crowd. So, with that, the fisherman gently eased
open a shell and slowly revealed the beautiful
secret hidden inside ...

... the most perfect, polished pearl that
shimmered and shone.
Everyone gasped in amazement.

"Look closely, Your Majesty, at the kaleidoscope of colours it holds," he whispered.
Everyone gasped even louder than the last time.
"I present to you the perfect gift for our perfect Queen. The best present ever," he exclaimed.

Everyone cheered and the King's face showed that he too had made up his mind.

"Yes, young man, this shall indeed be my gift," he announced.

Everyone cheered again (the loudest they'd ever cheered!), except for the other merchants from Africa, China and Russia, who were disappointed at not being chosen.

But the King had an idea and told them not to look so sad.

Several days later, the Queen was called
to the throne room to receive her gift.
She could hardly wait and excitedly
ripped open the gorgeous wrappings.
And there inside a box was ...

Can you guess?

The Queen loved her
present and hugged
the King saying,
"Perfect, just perfect,
the best present ever!"

Well, here is the portrait of the Queen that was painted soon afterwards. She was posing proudly wearing a beautiful silk dress, that gleamed with gold embroidery, dazzled with diamonds! And yes of course, teamed with stunning perfect pearls!

Later that year, in the month of June, a baby girl was born. In honour of the young fisherman and to show their gratitude to him, they named her...

Pearl.

"Princess Pearl.
Perfect," said
the fisherman.
"My best present
ever!" he beamed.